Firefighter Danny the Dog

Essential Fire Safety for Kids

Written by Benjamin C. Bak

Illustrated by Yousra Zekrifa

All Rights Reserved

© Copyright 2022 by Wordsmith Publishers - All rights reserved.

Without the prior written permission of the Publisher, no part of this publication may be stored in a retrieval system, replicated, or transferred in any form or medium, digital, scanning, recording, printing, mechanical, or otherwise, except as permitted under 1976 United States Copyright Act, section 107 or 108. Permission concerns should be directed to the publisher's permission department.

Legal Notice

This book is copyright protected. It is only to be used for personal purposes. Without the author's or publisher's permission, you cannot paraphrase, quote, copy, distribute, sell, or change any part of the information in this book.

Disclaimer Notice

This book is written and published independently. Please keep in mind that the material in this publication is solely for educational and entertaining purposes. All efforts have provided authentic, up-to-date, trustworthy, and comprehensive information. There are no express or implied assurances. The purpose of this book's material is to assist readers in having a better understanding of the subject matter. The activities, information, and exercises are provided solely for self-help information. This book is not intended to replace expert psychologists, legal, financial, or other guidance. If you require counseling, please get in touch with a qualified professional.

By reading this text, the reader accepts that the author will not be held liable for any damages, indirectly or directly, experienced due to the use of the information included herein, particularly, but not limited to, omissions, errors, or inaccuracies. As a reader, you are accountable for your decisions, actions, and consequences

Our fire station is so big that it can hold two huge fire trucks and three ambulances.
Upstairs, there are the offices and the break room. And what I love the most in this place is the slide! It is so much fun to slide on it. But it's not for playing; the firefighters use it to save time during emergencies like fire.

The fire is extremely dangerous; it is very hot and noisy. It creates a lot of smoke. It's so scary!
And it devours everything on its way, and spreads very quickly. That is why you always have to be careful when you are at home, and even at school.

Many things can cause fire in our home. Like the oven, candles, and even electricity.

That is why it is particularly important to have a smoke detector on every floor of your home, and check it each month, because that can really save your life.

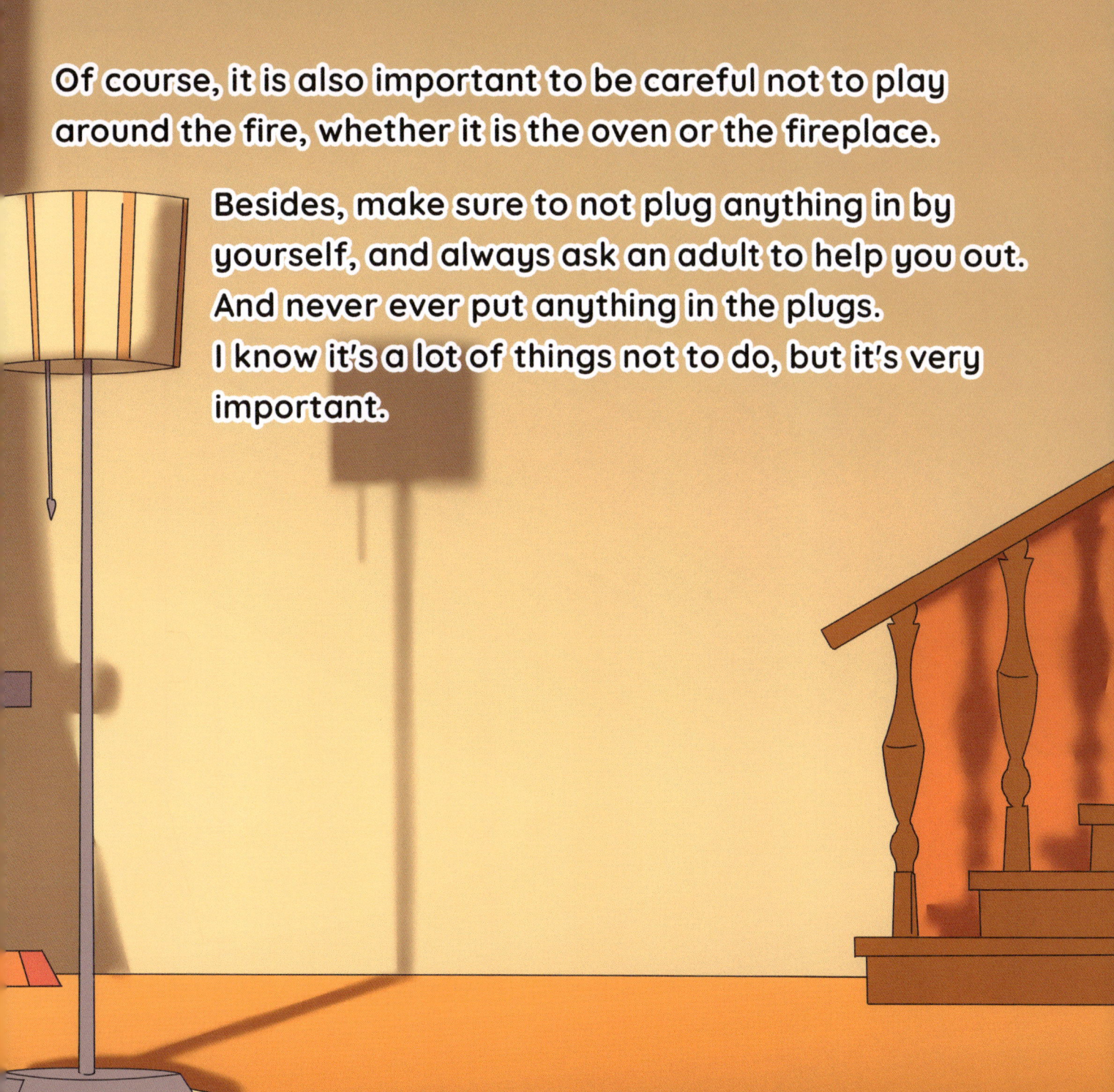

Of course, it is also important to be careful not to play around the fire, whether it is the oven or the fireplace.

Besides, make sure to not plug anything in by yourself, and always ask an adult to help you out. And never ever put anything in the plugs.
I know it's a lot of things not to do, but it's very important.

Now I am going to show you something. Can you guess what this is?

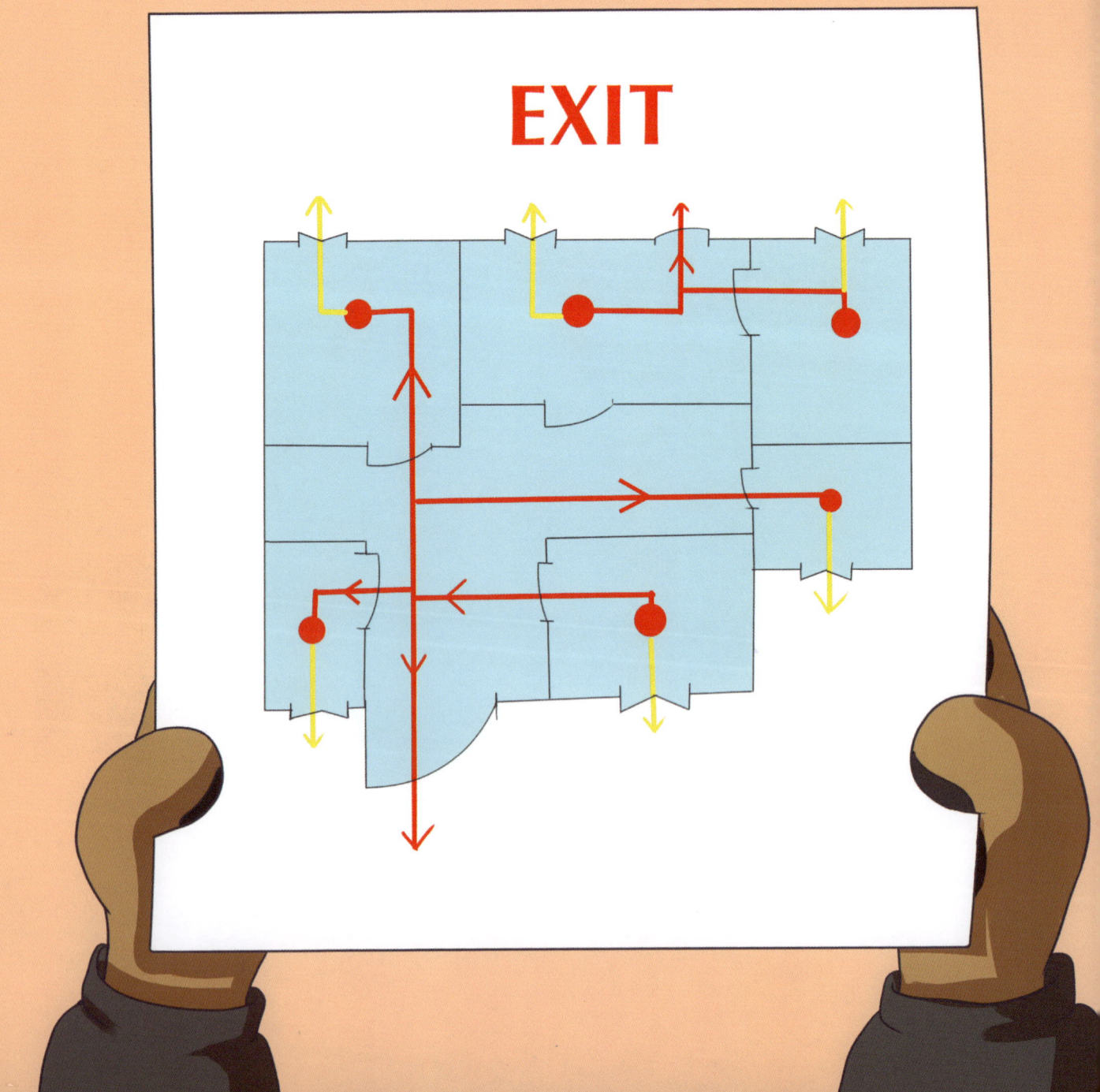

It is a fire escape plan of my house. You should ask your parents for an escape plan of your house too. You can even have fun practicing that exit plan with your family.

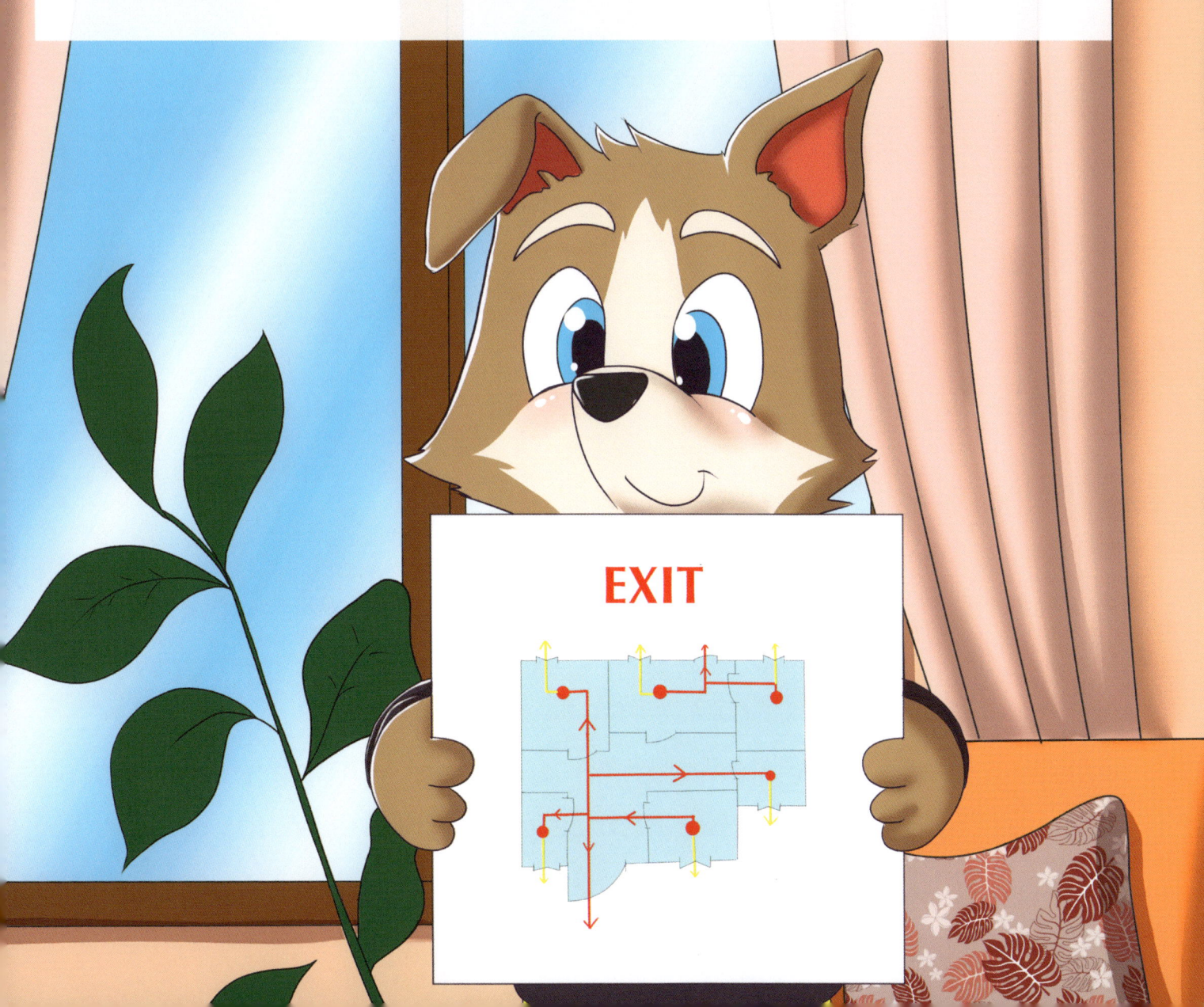

Now you might be thinking, "But Danny! What if there is a fire at home even with all these precautions. What should I do first?"

And that's a very smart question! The very first thing to do is to get outside of the house as quickly as possible, by following that exit plan you practiced with your family.

If there is, too much smoke in the house, get down on your knees and keep going forward. As the smoke rises to the top, the air below is more breathable.

Once you are outside and out of danger, do not go back in, even if you forgot your favorite stuffed animal inside. Then call 911 (US) or 112 (EU/UK) immediately.

However, if you are stuck in a room, do not open the door! That would make the fire spread into your room as well. And call for help. If you have a phone on you, call 911 (US) & 112 (EU/UK).

What you can do in the meantime, is to prevent the heat and smoke from coming through the door by blocking the cracks around the door with sheets or clothes. And wait for help to arrives to rescue you.

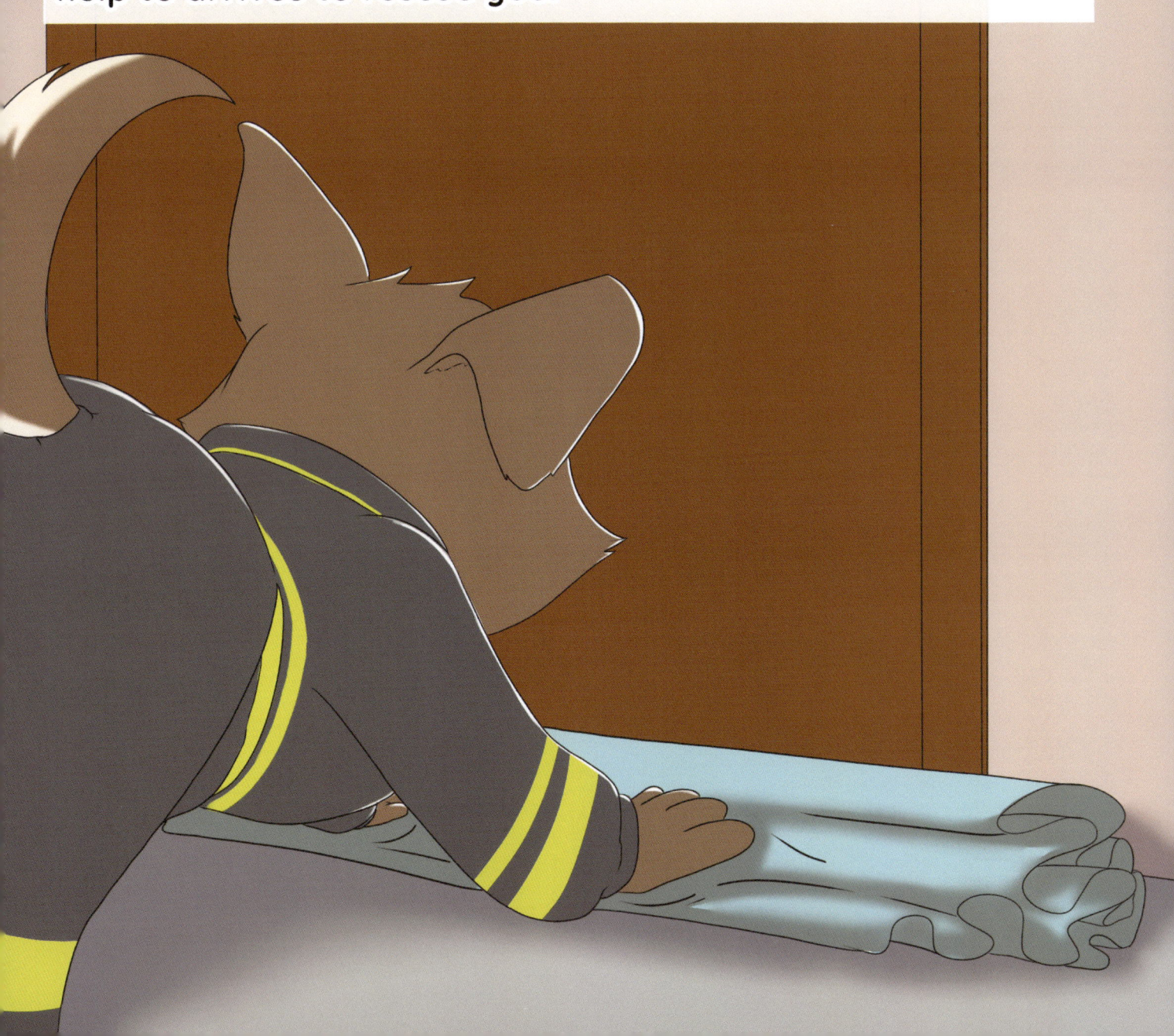

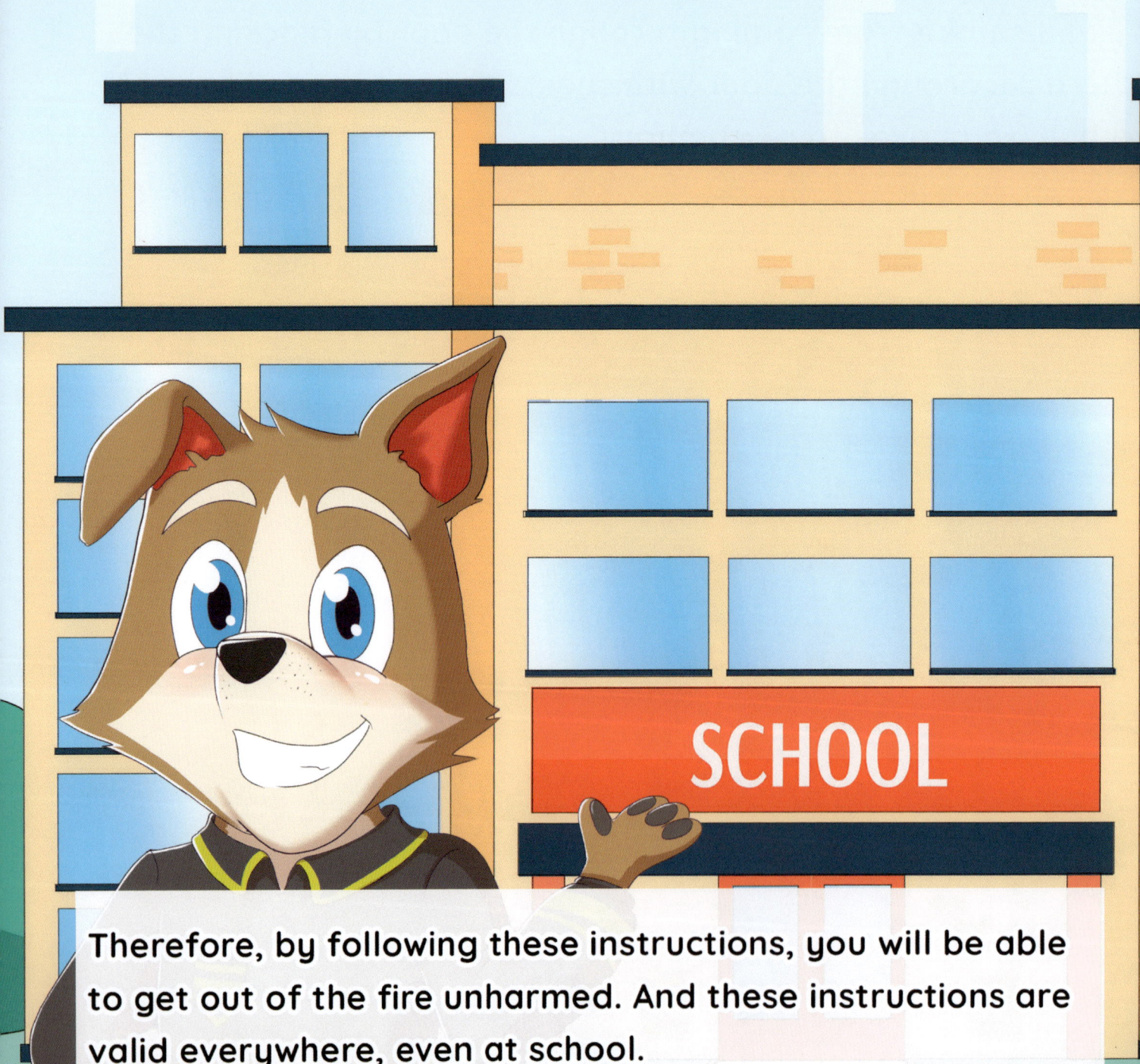

Therefore, by following these instructions, you will be able to get out of the fire unharmed. And these instructions are valid everywhere, even at school.

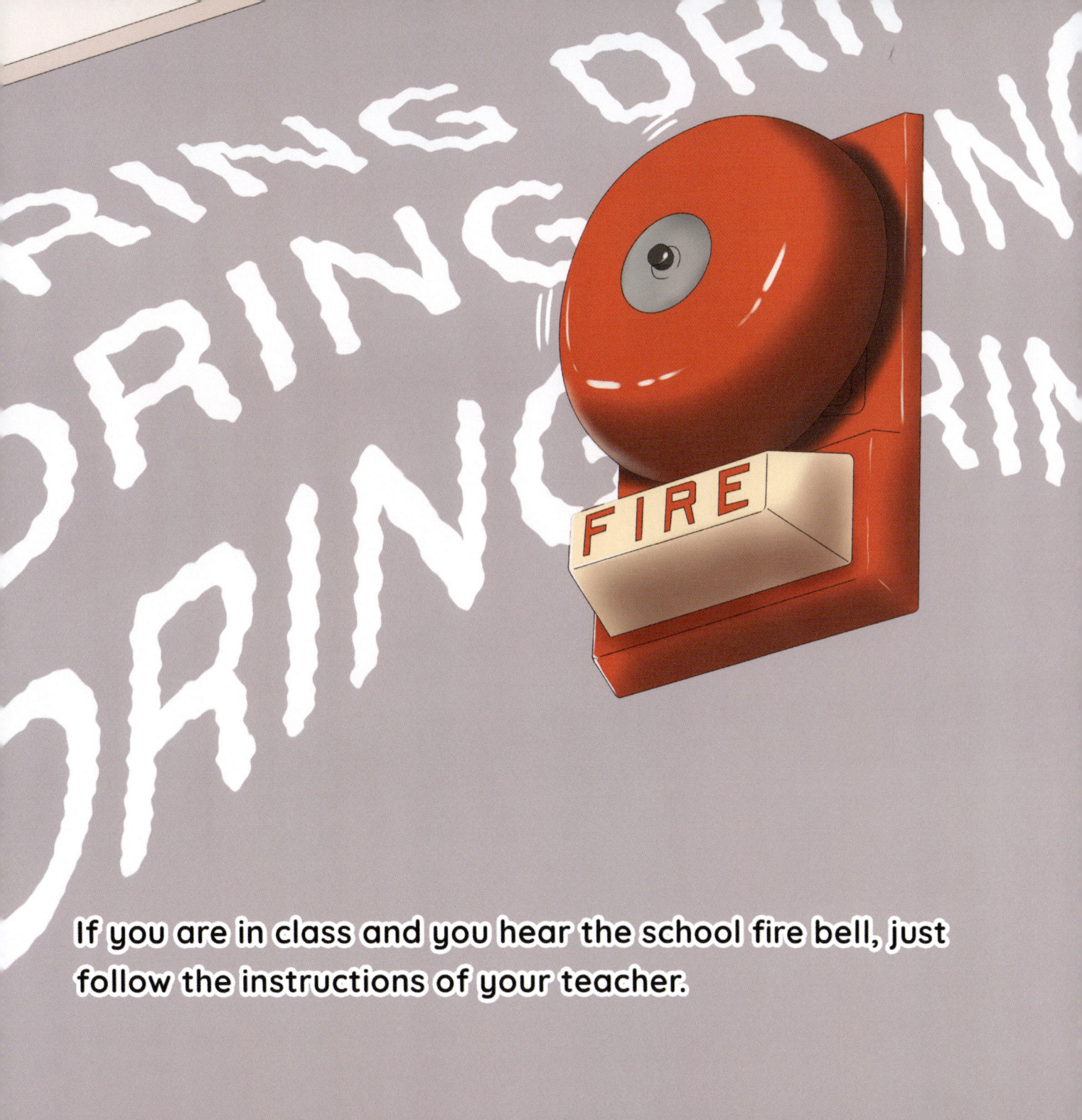

If you are in class and you hear the school fire bell, just follow the instructions of your teacher.

When evacuating, you must definitely not run, because that can cause many accidents. And if you are not in the classroom, just follow the exit plan by taking the nearest emergency exit and join your classmates as soon as you can.

Now my friend, we can say that you have become an expert in fire safety. I count on you to learn well what I taught you!

Oh look, a firefighter is ringing the bell; there must be a fire in the city! Duty awaits me! See you soon, I hope.
Take care of yourself and watch out for the fire!

What did you learn about Fire Safety

Can You find me?

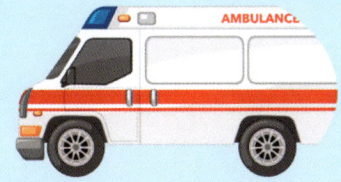
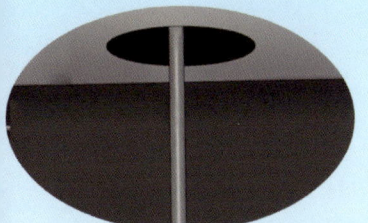

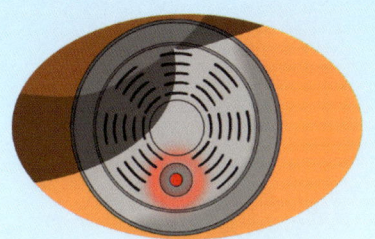
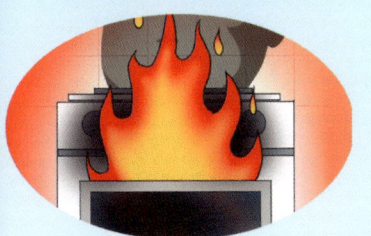
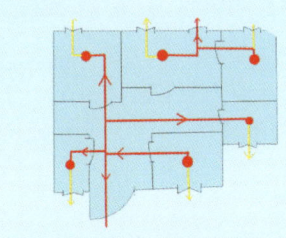
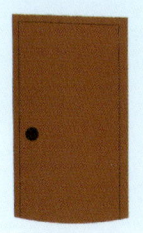

Printed in Great Britain
by Amazon